For dearest Brian,
who believed in my tree.

G.S.

In memory of Tom Calvert
who has his own little tree.

G.R.

Copyright © 2009 by Good Books, Intercourse, PA 17534
International Standard Book Number: 978-1-56148-663-2

Library of Congress Catalog Card Number: 2008038870

Text © Gillian Shields 2008
Illustrations © Gemma Raynor 2008

Original edition published in Great Britain in 2008 by
Gullane Children's Books,
185 Fleet Street, London, EC4A 2HS, England.

Printed in Indonesia

Library of Congress Cataloging-in-Publication Data

Shields, Gillian. Tom's tree / by Gillian Shields ; illustrated by Gemma Raynor. p. cm.
Summary: Tom plants a seed and imagines it growing into a giant tree with sturdy branches and a tree house,
while his brother Ned thinks it will never grow at all.
ISBN 978-1-56148-663-2 (hardcover : alk. paper)
[1. Trees--Fiction. 2. Growth--Fiction. 3. Imagination--Fiction.] I. Raynor, Gemma, ill. II. Title.
PZ7.S55478To 2009
[E]--dc22

2008038870

Tom's Tree

Gillian Shields

illustrated by
Gemma Raynor

Good Books

Intercourse , PA 17534
800/762-7171
www.GoodBooks.com

Tom planted a seed.
"That won't grow," laughed
his big brother Ned.

"I think it will," said Tom. "It will . . .

. . . grow into a tree with
strong green branches and
golden leaves and
red fruit and
peacocks singing."

"Peacocks don't sing," said Ned.

The next day, Tom looked where he had
planted the seed. There was no tree growing.
"Let's play soccer," said Ned.

But Tom was thinking about his tree.
"When my tree grows," he said, "we can . . .

. . . build a tree house
like a pirate ship and
fly over the moon."

"Trees can't fly," said Ned.

Every day Tom looked to
see if his tree was growing.
But the ground was
bare and empty.

"I told you so," said Ned.
Tom was sad.
"My tree would have been . . .

. . . as tall as a giant,
as wide as a rainbow and as strong as a dragon."

"Dragons don't exist," said Ned.

So Tom stopped hoping.

Then the winds came . . .

and the rain came . . .

and the snow and the frost,

until one day, the sun shone again . . .

. . . and the spring had come back.
"Look, Tom, look!" said Ned.
"It's your tree."

Tom smiled at Ned. Ned smiled at Tom.

"Pirates!"
"Dragons!"
"Rainbows!"
"Giants!"

"But," said Tom, looking at his tree again, "it's very small."

"Don't worry, it will soon grow," said Ned.

So Tom looked after
the tiny tree and watered it.

He built a little fence around it
so it wouldn't get damaged.

He watched and waited as a new shoot grew and fresh green buds opened.

At night Tom looked out of his
window into the darkness of the garden.
Sometimes he thought he could hear the
mast of a tall ship creaking in the wind
and the faint, soft sound of peacocks
singing under the starlight.

But every morning Tom's tree seemed as small as ever.
"I wish you'd hurry up," said Tom to the tree.

Spring followed spring.

Summer followed summer.

At last the tree grew, but Tom grew faster.

The day came when Tom was all grown up. He didn't think about pirates and dragons anymore. He went away to have grown-up adventures instead. The young, slim tree sighed in the breeze.

One day a man walked through the garden gate, down
the path and stood in front of the tree. It was Tom.
He was carrying his son on his shoulders.
"Look, Edward," said Tom. "This is my tree."
The tree was tall and wide, with strong green branches.

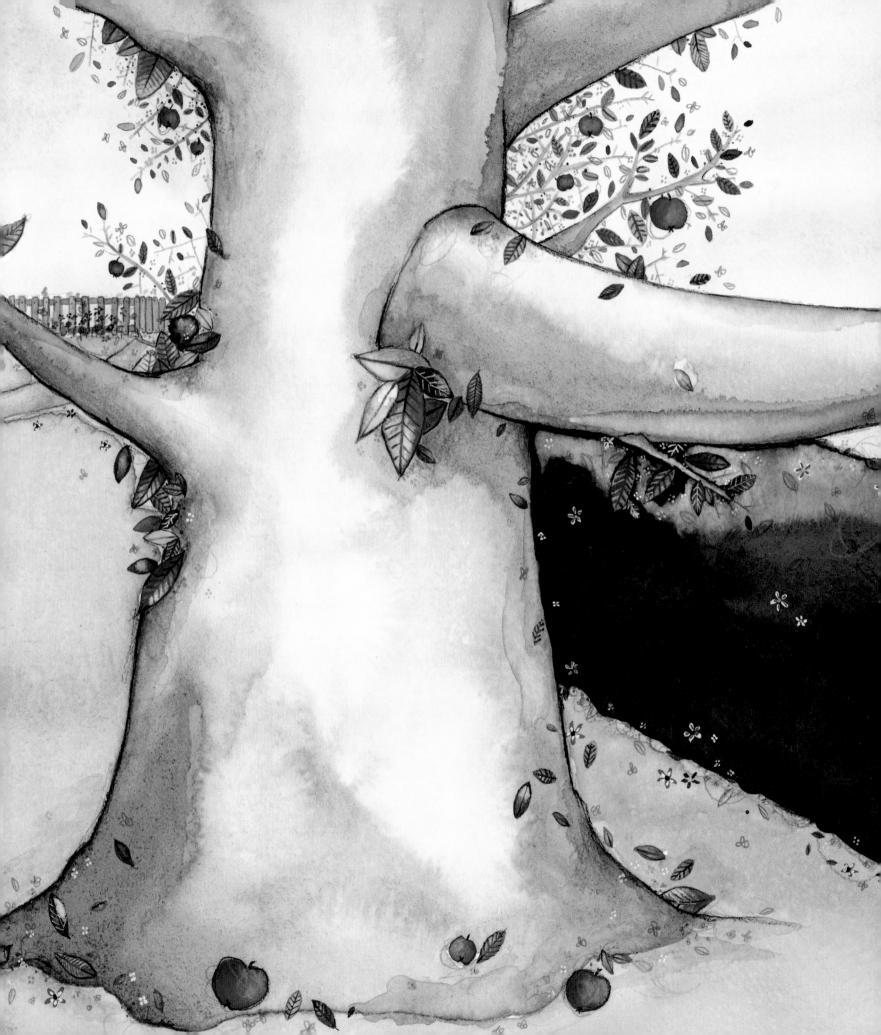

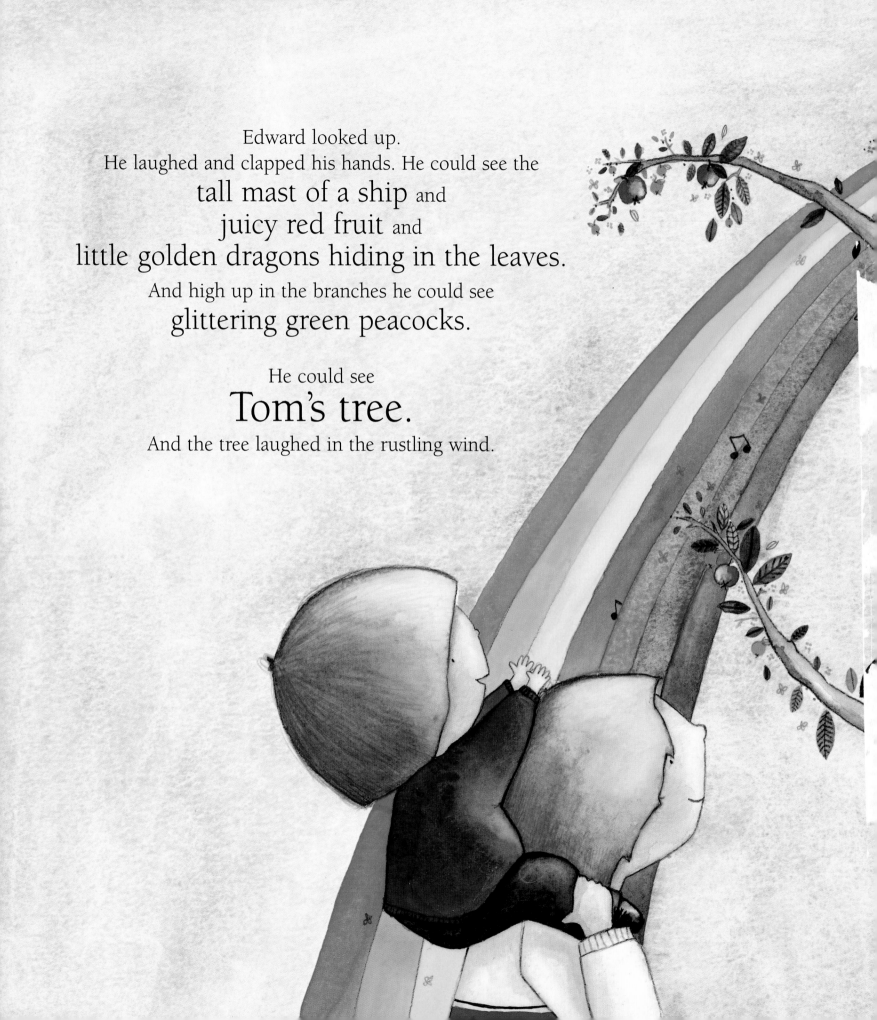

Edward looked up.
He laughed and clapped his hands. He could see the
tall mast of a ship and
juicy red fruit and
little golden dragons hiding in the leaves.
And high up in the branches he could see
glittering green peacocks.

He could see
Tom's tree.
And the tree laughed in the rustling wind.

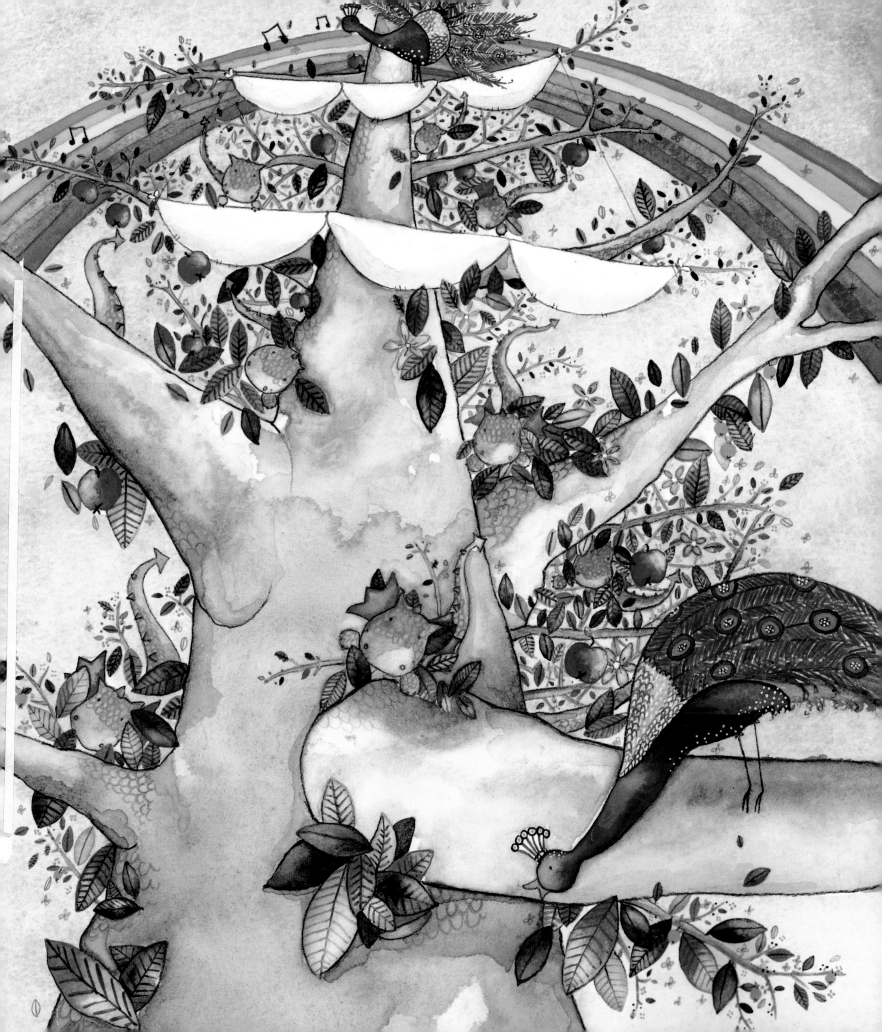